Santa's Ark

First published in the United States and Canada by
The Millbrook Press, Inc.
2 Old New Milford Road,
Brookfield, CT 06804

Devised and produced by
Tucker Slingsby Ltd,
Berkeley House,
73 Upper Richmond Road,
London SW15 2SZ

Library of Congress Cataloging-in-Publication Data

Wright, Cliff.
Santa's ark / by Cliff Wright.
        p.   cm.
Summary: A naughty little reindeer that wants to see the
world stows away aboard Santa's sleigh and invites other
baby animals to join him at each stop Santa makes.
  ISBN 0-7613-0299-9 (trade) ISBN 0-7613-0314-6 (lib. bdg.)
  [1. Reindeer—Fiction. 2. Animals—Fiction.
  3. Santa Claus—Fiction. 4. Christmas—Fiction.]   I. Title.
PZ7.W9347San   1997
[E]—dc21   97-11228
                                                                CIP
                                                                 AC

Printed in Singapore through Printlink International
Color reproduction by Bright Arts Graphics, Singapore

Santa's Ark

by Cliff Wright

The Millbrook Press, Inc.
Brookfield, Connecticut

It was Christmas Eve. The bright lights of
Santa's workshop shone across the snowy North Pole.
Santa gathered the reindeer together and harnessed
each one to his sleigh.

"Only the presents to load, and we're on our way!"
shouted Santa.

"Nearly ready," said Santa as he loaded the last and the biggest present onto the sleigh.

It was Santa's busiest night of the year. He was so busy that he didn't notice the little reindeer peeping through the window; so busy that he didn't see the little reindeer sneak through the door of his workshop.

Santa was so busy that he didn't notice the little reindeer creep onto the sleigh and hide under the presents. The stowaway was just in time. Santa's reindeer were already stamping their feet. Very soon they would be flying through the sky.

"Christmas crackers!" exclaimed Santa. "Off we go." And the reindeer raced across the snow until the sleigh rose into the twinkling sky.

As they soared among the frost-bright stars the little reindeer peeped out. A long, long way below, the snow sparkled with glittering lights.

To the little reindeer, the world looked like a great big Christmas cake. All the mountains and houses looked like toys. And Santa still didn't see his excited little passenger.

Whoosh! The sleigh swooped down and landed in the snow. As Santa went to deliver his first sack-load of presents the little reindeer poked his head up and then slipped out of the sleigh.

"Hello. Who are you?" asked a baby polar bear.

"I'm a reindeer and I'm off to see the world," he told the curious bear. "You can come too, but be quick, before Santa sees."

So the baby polar bear climbed aboard and the sleigh took off again. A seal watched the sleigh disappear into the night sky, and he wondered where it was going. For a minute, he wished he'd gone too.

They flew on. The sharp air roared in the little reindeer's ears and froze his nose—although the polar bear seemed to enjoy the frosty ride. The sleigh landed again, and Santa disappeared down a chimney.

A cat and a dog ran out of the house to see what was going on.

"Hello," said the little reindeer. "We're off to see the world. Why don't you come too? Quick, before Santa sees."

At first the cat and the dog were a little shy. The sleigh looked very exciting, but they weren't quite sure.

"We'll have great fun," said the little reindeer.

So the cat and dog jumped on board and the sleigh took off.

In Africa they landed with a bump. When the animals peeped out, they saw a baby elephant.

"Hello," said the little reindeer. "That's a big nose. What's it for?"

"This!" said the elephant and squirted them with water.

"Lovely!" they spluttered. "Come and see the world with us. Quick, before Santa sees." And together they heaved the elephant on board.

"Just one more push and you'll be in the sleigh," puffed the baby polar bear.

"Christmas crackers!" said Santa as they flew on. "This sleigh seems to be getting heavier and heavier."

Skimming over mountain tops, the sleigh stopped in China. There they saw a baby panda eating bamboo.

"We're off to see the world," they cried. "You can come too. Quick, before Santa sees."

So the panda clambered aboard Santa's sleigh and snuggled down.

The sleigh flew on to Australia and landed on a beach.

"Wow!" said the naughty little reindeer. "Look at those big waves. Let's surf!"

While Santa searched for chimneys and his team of reindeer snoozed, the little animals went surfing on the big blue waves.

On the beach they met a baby kangaroo.

"Hop on board and see the world with us. Quick, before Santa sees," said the little reindeer.

They flew on to the South Pole and landed near a penguin who was ice-sliding.

"Hello," said the penguin, "come and join in." So the little friends started sliding down the hill too. They were soon as warm as toast and having a great time.

"Come around the world
with us," said the little reindeer.
"Quick, before Santa sees."
The penguin stopped sliding,
and climbed into the sleigh.

The sleigh left the snowy wastes and flew above wild, green jungles. In a hot, steamy rainforest in South America, they saw a little monkey swinging from the trees by its tail.

"Hello," said the little reindeer, wishing he had a clever tail like that. "We're traveling around the world. Come with us. Quick, before Santa sees!"
So the monkey swung on board.

By now, the sleigh was very crowded.
"Christmas crackers!" exclaimed Santa as they flew on to North America. "I've delivered nearly all the presents, but my sleigh seems to be heavier than ever."

Miles high above New York, the little reindeer scrambled to get a good look at the Empire State Building. But he leaned too far and tumbled out of the sleigh. The polar bear, the dog and the cat, the panda, the kangaroo, the penguin, and the monkey fell after him. Only the little elephant clung onto the sleigh.

"Hang on, hang on!" she cried, and all the animals hung on with claws, paws, beaks, and tails. Then the elephant heaved and heaved and heaved again until she had pulled them all back into the sleigh. And still Santa did not see them.

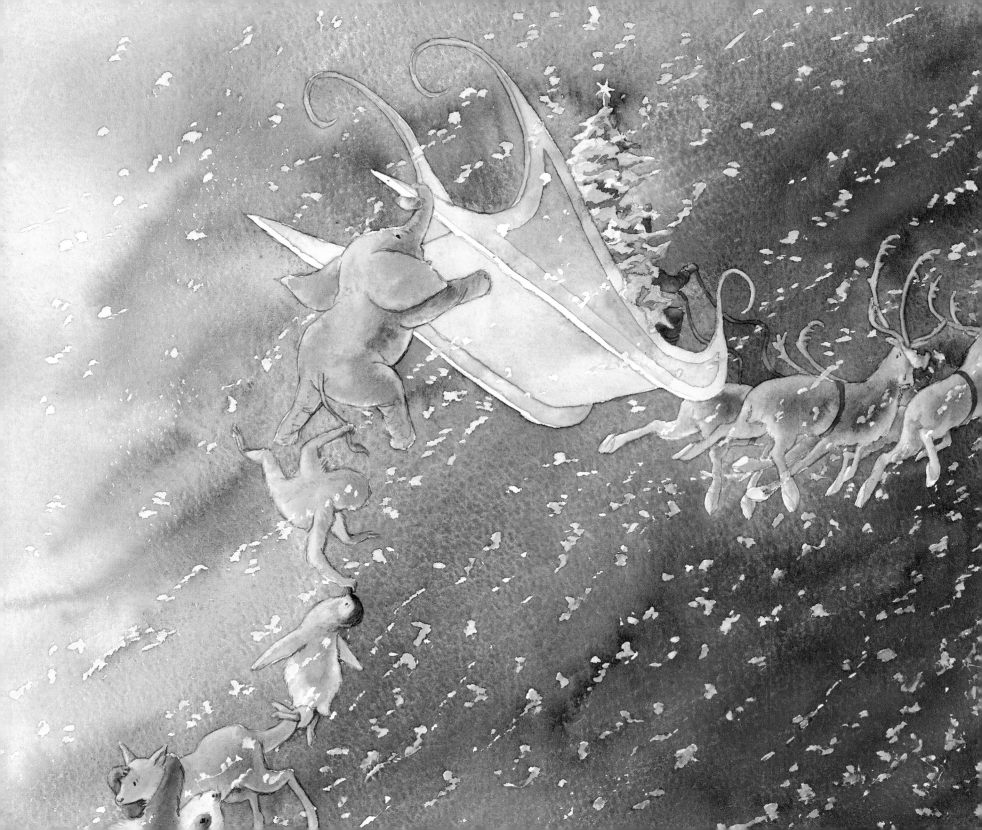

"All presents delivered," said Santa. "Time to go home,"
and he steered the big reindeer high over the ocean.
But they were very tired.
   "What's wrong, my friends?" Santa asked his reindeer.
   "It's the sleigh, Santa," they replied. "It's too heavy."

Santa turned around and nearly jumped out
of his skin. The sleigh was full of animals!
   "Jumping jingle bells!" shouted Santa.
   "It's not Santa's sleigh, it's Santa's ark!"
   They flew so slowly across the sky that
the sleigh went into a nose dive.

KER-SPLASH! went the sleigh as it hit the sea.
"Christmas crackers!" said Santa.
"That's done it. Mrs. Santa will be madder
than a melting snowman if we're not
home for breakfast."

Suddenly the sleigh was being lifted up and out of the sea.

"I'll take you home," boomed a voice nearby.

A baby whale had come to their rescue and all the stowaways climbed onto his back. The baby whale's mother swam alongside to keep them company.

The baby whale was so big that there was room on his back
for all the animals, Santa, and the sleigh too. There was much
excitement as they headed for the North Pole—and breakfast....

The dog and kangaroo danced while the panda gazed in wonder at the snowy mountains. Penguin was so excited he dived into the sea and swam on in front. Even the little reindeer was glad to be home.

Soon they were back at Santa's house. They were all very hungry and Mrs. Santa gave them a most magnificent breakfast. The little reindeer's mother peeped in at the window, happy to see her little stowaway safe and sound.

After a visit to Santa's workshop, the little friends were taken home to their families.

"You're a naughty little reindeer," said his mother when the others had left.
   "Sorry," said the tired young reindeer.
   "One day you'll be big enough to pull Santa's sleigh yourself, so don't sneak on board again," his mother told him.

It was Christmas morning
and the little reindeer knew Santa had
lots of presents waiting for him.
He was so excited. He couldn't wait to
open them, but he felt very sleepy....
Merry Christmas, little reindeer!

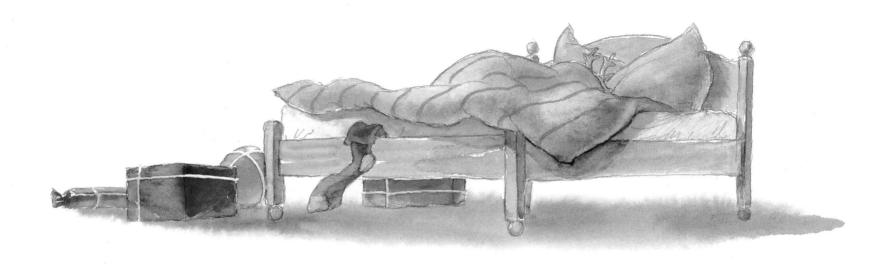